Ann Coburn has writ[ten]
for the stage and [is the]
author of several novels for older
children, including *Glint*, which
won an Arts Council Writer's
Award and a Northern Writer's
Award, and The Borderlands
Sequence, a quartet of novels that
also won an Arts Council Writer's
Award. Before becoming a full-
time writer, Ann worked as an
English teacher in an inner-city
comprehensive school. She has
given talks and run creative
writing workshops for children
and adults since her first novel
was published in 1991. Ann lives
in Northumberland.

You can find out more about
Ann and her books by visiting her
website, at www.anncoburn.com

WITHDRAWN FROM STOCK

Books by the same author

DreamTeam

"your dreams delivered"

Mission 1: Flying Solo

Ann Coburn

WALKER
BOOKS

Leabharlann Contae na Midhe

3585073

To Rosemary Canter,
for flying beside me

First published 2006 by Walker Books Ltd
87 Vauxhall Walk, London SE11 5HJ

2 4 6 8 10 9 7 5 3 1

Text © 2006 Ann Coburn
Illustrations © 2006 Garry Parsons

The right of Ann Coburn and Garry Parsons to be identified
as author and illustrator respectively of this work has been
asserted by them in accordance with the Copyright, Designs
and Patents Act 1988

This book has been typeset in Stone Informal

Printed and bound in China

All rights reserved. No part of this book may be reproduced,
transmitted or stored in an information retrieval system in any
form or by any means, graphic, electronic or mechanical,
including photocopying, taping and recording, without prior
written permission from the publisher.

British Library Cataloguing in Publication Data:
a catalogue record for this book is available
from the British Library

ISBN: 978-1-8442-8118-3

www.walker.co.uk

Contents

Wake-up Call

"**Stop!**" *ordered Vert.*

*Obediently, his dreamskoot slowed to a
halt and hovered in mid-air above the
rooftops of the Earthside town. Vert stood
up on the footrest and stared out to sea.
He had spotted something. A bank of fog as
grey and lumpy as cold porridge was rising*

from the water and rolling up the valley towards him. It was moving fast, flowing over even the highest buildings and blotting out the sky as it came.

Vert clenched his handsome square jaw and narrowed his steely blue eyes. If the fog caught him he would be flying blind. He turned to look at a hill on the other side of the valley. The gateway was on top of that hill, hidden away from human eyes inside an unremarkable pile of stones. The gateway was his way home to the safety of Dreamside, but first he had to reach the hilltop – and that meant flying across the path of the fog.

Vert put his head down and opened up the throttle. His dreamskoot shot towards the hill, skimming over the rooftops like a rocket-powered moth. He was nearly there when the fog caught him. Vert switched on his headlight. The beam hit the wall of fog and bounced right back at him. He sighed and looked down at the dreamskoot's control panel. He would have to rely on his navigation screens.

A squawk made Vert look up again. A huge crow had come flapping out of the fog and was heading straight for him. The crow tried to change direction but it was too late. A glossy black wing knocked Vert sideways in the saddle and sharp claws raked his dreamskoot from tip to tail. Then the crow was gone, swallowed up by the fog again.

Vert had lost his grip on the handlebars and he only had one leg hooked over his saddle. He tried to clamber back onto his dreamskoot, but the little machine tipped over and fell away from him like a stone. Its silvery wings had been ripped to shreds. Vert tumbled after his dreamskoot, falling helplessly towards the ground. He opened his mouth …

…and screamed.
Vert's eyes
snapped open and
his body gave a
huge jump. He sat
bolt upright and
gazed wildly about
him. He was not
falling from a great
height. He was safe in his bed in the
dormitory. Vert stopped screaming,
pushed back the covers and swung his
trembling legs over the side of the bed.
He caught sight of himself in the mirror
on the side of Snaffle's locker and shook
his head at what he saw. The real Vert
was nothing like the dream Vert. His
jaw was not square and handsome, but
a bit weak and wobbly. His almond-
shaped eyes were not steely blue but a
gentle green. His nicely pointed ears

were his only good feature, but this
morning they were hidden under
the wild tangle his hair had become
overnight. He was a mess. Vert groaned
and slumped back onto his bed. He was
never going to make it as a Dream
Fetcher.

"Honestly," said a sneery voice. "It's
like sharing a dorm with a faulty fire
alarm."

Hastily, Vert wiped
the sweat from his face
and propped himself
up on one elbow.
Snaffle was standing
by the door at the end
of the dormitory.

"Every morning the
same," sneered
Snaffle.

"What?" said Vert.

"You scream the place down, that's what!" said Snaffle. "It's so embarrassing. I wish you weren't in my dream team. They're starting to call us the Scream Team."

"Sorry. I had another nightmare," said Vert.

"What about?"

"Can't remember," muttered Vert, pulling the covers over his head so Snaffle would not see that he was lying. Ever since he had started training to be a Dream Fetcher, Vert had been having nightmares. They always ended the same way, with him falling out of the sky. Vert had not told anyone about the nightmares in case they guessed his terrible secret. No one, not even Team Leader Flint, knew what that secret was. The truth was, Vert was afraid of heights. No. That was not quite right.

Vert was afraid of flying. He was terrified of being up in the air with nothing but his dreamskoot beneath him. He could not quite believe that the gossamer-thin wings were strong enough to hold him up.

Suddenly, Vert's eyes widened in horror. He had just remembered what day it was. After six weeks of basic training, he, Snaffle, Harley and Midge were about to fly their first real missions. They would each be going Earthside to make a solo dream delivery. Team Leader Flint had told them to report to the Dream Centre straight after breakfast. Vert threw back the covers and looked over at the dormitory window. Daylight was streaming in. He had overslept!

"Why didn't you wake me?" he gasped, scrambling out of bed.

"I don't do wake-up calls," said Snaffle.

Vert looked more closely at his team mate. Snaffle was fully dressed in his trainee Dream Fetcher uniform, but he wasn't wearing any boots. Behind him, the dormitory door stood half open. Vert looked at Snaffle accusingly.

"You were sneaking out in your socks so you wouldn't wake me!"

"And I very nearly made it," said Snaffle, bringing his helmet out from under his arm. His boots were wedged inside. "But then the stupid door hinge squeaked." He pulled his boots from the helmet and began to put them on. "Pity. I wanted you to oversleep."

"But – why?" asked Vert. "We're on the same dream team, aren't we?"

Snaffle sneered. "You still don't get it, do you?" he said, balancing on one leg to put a boot on.

"Get what?" asked Midge, poking her head into the dormitory. Snaffle jumped and nearly fell over. Midge giggled.

"Get lost, Shorty," snapped Snaffle, stamping his foot into his boot. "I wasn't talking to you."

Midge stopped smiling. All through their basic training she had tried to be friends with Snaffle. After all, they were on the same dream team. But sometimes Snaffle was very hard to like. He had a nasty way of knowing just how to upset a person – and "Shorty" was the worst name to call Midge. She hated being so small.

Midge had always longed to be a Dream Fetcher. Dream Fetchers had been delivering dreams to humans ever since the first dream orders started coming through, back in the Stone Age. Midge wanted to be a part of that long tradition.

As soon as she was old enough, she had started applying to join a dream team, but Team Leader Flint had always rejected her. The problem was, a Dream Fetcher was supposed to be at least seven centimetres tall. Midge had stopped growing at six and three quarter centimetres. But she would not give up. She had kept on applying until finally it had happened. Midge had been standing at the height chart yet again, stretching her neck and struggling to stay up on her toes. Team Leader Flint had stared at her for the longest time, looking right into her eyes. Midge had stared back, full of determination. Finally, Team Leader Flint had nodded and ticked her clipboard. Midge had made it through at last.

And now Snaffle, one of her own team mates, was calling her "Shorty"! Midge stood as tall as she could and stepped forward. "What did you say?"

Snaffle did not even look round. "You heard me, Shorty," he said, pulling on his other boot. "And if you take one more step into this room, I'll report you. Girls aren't allowed in the boys' dorm."

Midge stepped back into the corridor and glared at Snaffle's back.

"What is it I don't get?" asked Vert quickly, seeing that Midge was about to lose her temper with Snaffle.

"What you don't get," said Snaffle, "is that this is a competition."

"It is?" said Vert.

"Yes! We might all be on the same team, but we're not on the same side. Team Leader Flint will be scoring us on each training mission. And I'm going for the highest pass mark. I'm planning to beat you all. So, Vert, of course I'm not going to wake you up when you oversleep. If you lose points, that helps me. See?"

"Not really," said Vert. "I think we should be on the same side."

Snaffle gave a short, hard laugh. Vert hung his head and looked so hurt that Snaffle felt a twinge of guilt. Quickly, he pictured the smug face of his older brother Grabble and the twinge of guilt vanished. Two years earlier, Grabble had graduated with the highest score ever awarded to a trainee Dream Fetcher. Now he was well on the way to becoming the youngest Team Leader in the history of the service.

Snaffle scowled and clenched his fists. He had to beat Grabble's score. Then perhaps his parents would be proud of him, too. Snaffle turned away from the hurt look on Vert's face, pushed past Midge and marched off along the corridor.

"I'm sure he loves us really," sighed Midge, stepping into the dormitory as soon as Snaffle was out of sight.

"I feel sorry for him," said Vert. "He never smiles. Have you noticed?"

"I've noticed that you're not dressed yet," said Midge, pulling Vert's uniform from his locker. "And your hair! Come on. We still have time. You'll have to miss breakfast, though."

Vert felt his stomach heave at the very thought of food. "I'm not hungry," he gulped and changed the subject. "Where's Harley?"

"Guess," smiled Midge.

Harley was outside on the dreamskoot training range, hard at work. The
training range was an enormous obstacle
course. It was where trainee Dream
Fetchers learned how to handle their
dreamskoots before flying Earthside
missions for real. Most trainees hated the
tough dreamskoot range. Harley loved it.
She spent most of her spare time out
there, putting her dreamskoot through its
paces. She had already broken the course
record for the fastest time. Now she was

trying to beat her own best score.

Harley shot across the finish line, turned her dreamskoot neatly in mid-air and brought it to a stop. She hovered, waiting for her latest score to appear on the screen outside the supervisor's cabin. The numbers flashed up and a group of Dream Fetchers who had stopped to watch gave her a round of applause. Harley shrugged. She didn't see much to clap about. She had shaved a measly tenth of a second off her previous best time.

"Again, please," she said, speaking into the mouthpiece of the dreamcom inside her helmet.

"Absolutely not," snapped the training range supervisor into Harley's earpiece. "You don't have time to do another run. You should be reporting to the Dream Centre right now!"

Leabharlann 3585073 Contae na Mídhe

"Just one more try, sir," said Harley. "Please?"

The supervisor sighed into Harley's earpiece. Then her latest score disappeared from the screen, and the light above the starting line turned from red to green. Harley grinned and leaned forward over her handlebars. As she waited for the countdown to begin, she glanced at her audience of Dream Fetchers. They were all slightly older than her and she could tell by their uniforms that they were fully qualified. Well, she might be only a trainee, but she would show them something about flying! One of the Dream Fetchers, the one with the grey eyes and narrow mouth, caught her attention. He looked strangely familiar.

"Five … four…"

As the countdown began, Harley

settled herself more firmly into the saddle and stopped trying to figure out who the grey-eyed Dream Fetcher was. Out of the corner of her eye she could see Midge and Vert waving to her as they walked towards the training range, but she did not wave back. She kept her hands firmly on the handlebars.

"...three ... two..."

Harley stared at the long line of obstacles ahead of her, going over the quickest route in her head.

"...one ... zero!"

Harley opened up the throttle. Her dreamskoot raced towards the first obstacle. It was an Earthside window, built to human scale, which meant that it was taller than most Dreamside buildings. The top part of the window was unlatched, but it kept opening and shutting, as though a strong Earthside

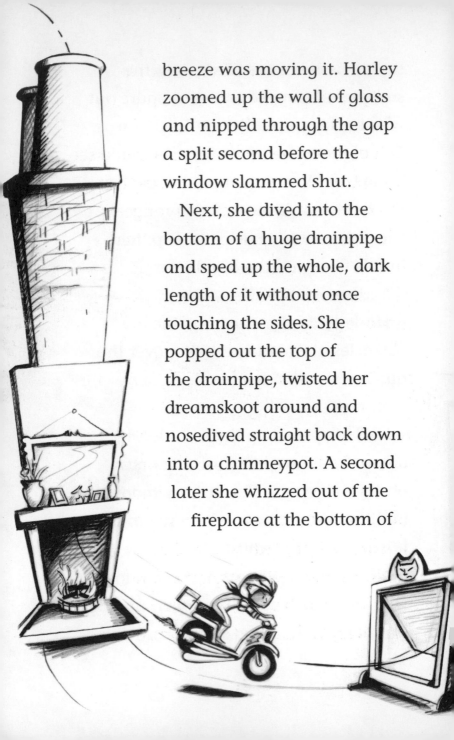

breeze was moving it. Harley
zoomed up the wall of glass
and nipped through the gap
a split second before the
window slammed shut.

Next, she dived into the
bottom of a huge drainpipe
and sped up the whole, dark
length of it without once
touching the sides. She
popped out the top of
the drainpipe, twisted her
dreamskoot around and
nosedived straight back down
into a chimneypot. A second
later she whizzed out of the
fireplace at the bottom of

the chimney and headed straight for
a huge catflap.

Wham!

The nose of her dreamskoot slammed
into the corner of the flap, hitting just
the right spot. The catflap flew open.
Harley shot through and immediately
turned sharp right to avoid the
realistic cat paw that tried to swat
her out of the air.

The next obstacle was a
huge wall fan. Harley brought
her dreamskoot to a stop in front of it.
Whump, whump, whump. The arms of the
fan turned steadily. Harley nodded her
head as she counted them off. Timing
was everything with this obstacle. She

took a deep breath and, after one more *whump*, guided her dreamskoot through the slats and into the fan. She eased out the other side just before the next arm whumped past behind her. Harley let out her breath. The most difficult bit was over now. She made short work of the elevator ride, the spring-loaded letter box and the sliding doors before putting her head down and racing for the finish line.

Midge and Vert cheered and the grey-eyed Dream Fetcher looked at her with grudging admiration. Harley knew she had done well, but what was her time? Everyone went quiet and turned to the scoreboard. The sound of approaching footsteps was loud in the silence.

"What's going on?" said Snaffle, coming up behind Midge and Vert.

He did not get an answer. Suddenly everyone was too busy cheering. Harley's score had appeared. She had beaten her previous time by over a second!

"I said, what's going on?" demanded Snaffle, poking Midge in the back as Harley brought her dreamskoot in to land. Midge turned to explain, but Snaffle was no longer paying attention to her. He had just spotted the grey-eyed Dream Fetcher. His face lit up with happiness.

"Grabble!" he cried. "You came! And Mum and Dad too? Where are they?" Eagerly he looked around and then turned back to his big brother.

"What are you talking about?" said Grabble.

"It's my first solo flight today," said Snaffle, beginning to look unsure. "That is why you're here, isn't it? To see me off?"

Grabble laughed. "Why would Mum and Dad travel all the way here for a solo flight?" he scoffed. "It's no big deal, little brother."

"Ha, ha, ha!" laughed Snaffle through gritted teeth. "No big deal. I knew that."

"I just brought my dreamskoot in for a service," said Grabble. "And I stopped to watch the show. This guy is really good. Do you know who he is?"

"It's not a guy," snapped Snaffle, glowering at Harley. "It's a girl. She's in my dream team." Harley pulled her helmet off and her long black hair came tumbling down.

"You mean even the girls in your dream team are better than you, Snaffle?" smirked Grabble.

"Oh, I'm not the best in our team," said Harley, pressing the homing button on her dreamskoot. The little machine rose into the air and hummed away, heading for Harley's launch pad in the Dream Centre. "Who do you think taught me to fly like that? Your little brother, that's who," she fibbed, looking Grabble straight in the eye. Grabble's narrow mouth dropped open.

Snaffle glowered even harder as Harley put an arm around his shoulder, but he could say nothing while Grabble was watching.

"That sorted *him* out," muttered Harley from the corner of her mouth. "Come on, Dream Team," she added, in a louder voice. "We have an Earthside mission to complete."

Midge and Vert came up on either side of Snaffle and Harley. All four of them strode off towards the Dream Centre, walking in step, with their helmets tucked under their arms and their shadows stretching out behind them.

The Dream Team was ready for action.

Breaking the Rules

Midge stood back and inspected her dreamskoot. She had not stopped dusting and polishing since Team Leader Flint had picked her to fly first, and now the little machine gleamed under the launch-pad lights. The chrome sparkled, the paintwork shone and there was not a speck of dust on the saddle or footplates. Midge rubbed a tiny smear from the windscreen with the sleeve of her uniform jacket and then allowed

herself a tiny smile. Perfect. Her dreamskoot was ready. But was *she*? She
tugged at her uniform and checked the
shine on her boots.

"Relax, kiddo," drawled Harley from
the next launch pad. "We'll be OK.
Flying solo is no big deal."

Midge looked over at her friend.
Harley did not seem at all nervous.
She was lying along the saddle of her
dreamskoot. Her feet were up on the
handlebars and her hands were tucked
behind her head.

"It *is* a big deal," said Midge. "For me."

Midge gazed around the busy Dream Centre. It had taken her so long to get this far, and she knew there was nowhere she would rather be. It was a huge place, full of noise and lights. Behind her was the switchboard room, where all incoming dream orders were logged and sorted. Next to the switchboard room were the steamy kitchens, where teams of Dream Chefs prepared the dreams for delivery. The dreamskoot garages and repair workshops were beside the kitchens and, rising high above them all, was the Dream Traffic Control Tower.

Midge looked up at the Control-Tower windows. Her mum and dad were up there with all the other Dream Traffic Controllers. They were sitting in front of

rows of monitors, watching hundreds of green dots move across their screens. Each dot marked the location of a Dream Fetcher making an Earthside dream delivery. Midge smiled as she remembered that soon she would be one of the green dots on the monitor screens.

Clang, clang, clang!

Midge froze. That was the sound of Team Leader Flint's steel-tipped boots hitting the launch-pad walkway.

Clang, clang, clang!

Midge risked a quick sideways glance. Team Leader Flint was right at the far end of the long line of launch pads. There was still time for Midge to warn the other three.

She turned to Harley first. Harley had pulled her neckerchief up over her eyes. She seemed to be asleep.

"Harley!" hissed Midge. "Wake up!

Flint is on her way with my delivery!"

Harley rose to her feet in one smooth movement. Midge looked past Harley to the next launch pad. Where was Vert? He should have been standing next to his dreamskoot but he was nowhere in sight.

Clang, clang, clang!

Midge glanced over her shoulder. Team Leader Flint was much closer now. She was striding towards them, striking sparks from the metal floor with every step.

Snaffle was standing to attention next to his dreamskoot. He looked very smart – and very smug.

"Where's Vert gone?" hissed Midge, looking at Snaffle. Snaffle shrugged.

Then Midge spotted him. Vert was at the kitchen serving hatch again, chatting to the Dream Chefs.

"He's behind you, Snaffle!" hissed

Midge. "Quick! Warn him before he gets into trouble!"

Snaffle pretended not to understand.

"Come on, Snaffle!" snapped Harley, out of the corner of her mouth. "You're the closest!"

"Pardon?" said Snaffle.

Clang, clang, CLANG!

Team Leader Flint had arrived. Vert did not notice. He was leaning across the serving counter, with his head in the kitchens and his bottom sticking up in the air. Team Leader Flint folded her arms and stared at Vert's bottom. "*Mister Vert!*" she yelled.

Vert jumped up and hurried back to his launch pad.

"Did you see any dreams being made?" asked Team Leader Flint.

"N-no," quavered Vert.

"Are you sure? You're flying today," said Team Leader Flint, pointing up at the space above the launch pads. The Three Abiding Rules were written there in letters of gold.

1. `Always` deliver what the customer orders

2. `Don't` look inside the BOX

3. `Never` be SEEN

Vert read the second Abiding Rule and gulped. He understood what Team Leader Flint was asking. He should not have been anywhere near the kitchens just before a flight in case he saw the dream he would be delivering. A Dream Fetcher caught deliberately breaking any of the Abiding Rules was dismissed. No questions. No exceptions.

"I was only having a chat with the chefs," said Vert. "I didn't see any dreams being made. Honest."

Team Leader Flint gave Vert a steely look and made a mark on her clipboard. Snaffle smirked.

"Ready?" asked Flint, turning to Midge.

"Yes, boss," said Midge, saluting smartly.

Flint nodded. "Activate!" she ordered. The face of a human boy appeared on the screen above Midge's launch pad. "Johnny Davis," said Flint, reading from the screen. "An eight-year-old male. His order will be ready any minute."

Midge grinned with excitement as she swung herself up onto the dreamskoot. Her very first customer! Settling into the saddle, Midge pressed her thumb against the identity pad on the control panel. She felt a tingle as the dreamskoot scanned her thumbprint. The screen in the middle of the control panel lit up and words began to appear.

Welcome, Midge, said the screen. *Ready to go?*

"Power up, please," said Midge.

All the lights on the control panel flickered on. Midge nodded with satisfaction. Everything was fully charged. She turned the handlebar throttle just a bit. Her dreamskoot rose into the air. It hovered a few inches above the launch pad, tugging at its anchor ropes.

"Oh dear," said Harley.

"What's wrong?" asked Midge.

"Here comes Johnny's order," said Harley. "It's a nightmare."

Midge's grin disappeared. She turned to look. One of the Dark Side chefs was scurrying towards her launch pad. His chef's hat and jacket were deep black. His skin was pale and he was blinking in the glare of the launch-pad lights. Without a word, he pushed a flat, square cardboard box into the padded holder on Midge's dreamskoot. Then he hurried back to the gloomy Dark Side of the kitchens.

Midge stared down at the box. Black oily stains were spreading across the cardboard. A sour green steam rose from the stains. The nightmare inside must be very bad. Midge looked at Johnny's face on the launch-pad screen. She bit her lip.

Slam! Team Leader Flint snapped shut the lid of the padded holder. "Midge!" she warned. "Remember the first Abiding Rule. Always deliver what the customer orders."

Midge sighed. Every Dream Fetcher had to obey the Three Abiding Rules. Without question. She put on her helmet, leant forward over the saddle and gripped the handlebars.

"Good luck," said Vert and Harley. Snaffle just sneered.

"Lift off!" ordered Midge.

Her dreamskoot rose into the air.

"Wings out!"

Two fan-shaped wings opened out from beneath the footplates. They shimmered with silvery light.

"Earthside!" ordered Midge, opening the throttle.

Her dreamskoot surged forward and headed straight for the far wall of the Dream Centre. An enormous circular steel frame was set into the wall. A thin skin was stretched across the frame. It was full of changing colours, like the liquid in a huge bubble wand. This was the gateway between Dreamside and Earthside.

Midge hit the gateway. At first it felt as though she had flown into a

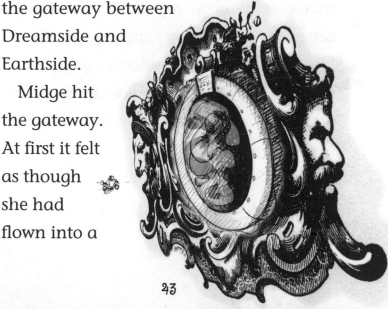

plate of warm jelly. Then it felt as though she *were* the jelly, being pushed through a sieve. Finally, she burst through into the cold night air of Earthside.

Stars twinkled above her, and the streets of the Earthtown were spread out below. Midge went into a dive, whooping with excitement as her dreamskoot shot through the darkness. She had been Earthside before, but never on her own. She pulled out of the dive and hovered just above the Town Hall roof. Her job now was to deliver Johnny's order while it was still crisp and hot. Midge looked at the street map on her dreamskoot screen. There were three dots on the map. The red dot was Johnny's house. The green dot was her dreamskoot. The blue dot marked the gateway that would take her back to

Dreamside once she had completed her delivery.

Midge set off, skimming over the heads of the few humans still out on the streets below. Not one of them spotted her. Even if a human did glance up, Midge knew they would look at the underside of her dreamskoot and think she was a very large moth, or a scrap of paper blowing in the wind. On she went, peeking into shop windows and dodging double-decker buses. She was trying to enjoy her first solo trip, but it was hard to forget what was in the box on the back of her dreamskoot.

The closer she got to Johnny's house, the worse Midge felt. Team Leader Flint said that nightmares weren't all bad.

Sometimes they helped humans face up to the things they feared. Still, Midge wished her first delivery had been a dream.

Johnny's house was in a quiet, terraced street. The top part of his bedroom window was slightly open. Midge hovered outside the window, looking in. A lamp had been left on in the room. Johnny was asleep and there were no dogs, cats or parents in sight. Midge eased her dreamskoot inside and then flew over to Johnny's bed. She turned in the saddle and lifted the delivery box out of the padded holder. Now all she had to do was swoop down and make the dream-drop. As long as the box landed somewhere on Johnny's body, the nightmare would sink into him.

Midge hesitated. Johnny was sleeping

so peacefully. She looked around his room. She saw packing cases stacked in the corner. A new school uniform was spread out on a chair beside Johnny's bed. Midge had paid attention in all her Human Studies lessons. She knew what the packing cases and the uniform meant. Johnny had just moved house and he would be starting a new school in the morning. His whole life had changed overnight. He must be feeling very scared. No wonder his brain had ordered a nightmare.

But would this nightmare help or make things worse? Perhaps she should just check. Midge looked down at the box in her hand. She bit her lip. The second Abiding Rule could not be any clearer. Don't look inside the box. Midge shook her head and sat up straight. She knew the penalty for deliberately breaking an Abiding Rule. If caught, she would be dismissed from the service. Did she really want to risk that? No. It was time to make the drop and head back to Dreamside. She gripped the box in one hand and steered her dreamskoot towards the head of the bed. Just then, Johnny turned over onto his back and Midge got her first good look at his face. He was very sweet, for a human.

Midge faltered to a stop and hovered above the pillow, glancing between the sleeping boy and the dream box she was carrying. Perhaps just one peek. No one would know. She lifted a corner of the box lid and peeked at the circle of baked dream-dough inside. The toppings on the dream-crust were a nasty mixture of green dread, black fear and purple panic. Midge took a sniff of the steam rising from the box and caught a glimpse of Johnny's nightmare. She saw Johnny running down endless school corridors in the dark. He was lost and scared. There were monsters waiting in the shadows.

Midge gave a horrified squeak and slammed the box lid shut. She had seen enough. This nightmare would not help Johnny's fears about starting a new school. It would make them ten times worse. What was she going to do?

Below her, Johnny made a noise. His eyelids began to flutter. He was waking up! Midge swooped down towards his face. If she made her delivery in time, the nightmare would send him back to sleep. Midge flew in and prepared to make the drop but, at the last second, she swerved away again. She could not give Johnny this nightmare. Instead, she dropped the box over the side of the bed

and watched it fall to the floor. *Phut!*
The nightmare disappeared with a tiny
fizzle. Midge nodded. She could say it
was an accident. A fumbled dream-drop.

Then she looked up and screamed. Her
dreamskoot was heading straight for
the bedroom wall. Midge forced it
into a tight turn and then pulled
up on the handlebars. The
dreamskoot shot upwards,
skimming the wall so closely that
Midge could have reached out
and touched the wallpaper.
Slowly, slowly the
dreamskoot turned
away from the
wall and
levelled out.

As soon as she was out of danger, Midge came to a halt, yanked off her helmet and wiped her face with a shaking hand.

"Hello."

Midge nearly fell off her dreamskoot. She turned around. Johnny was propped up on one elbow, gazing at her with sleepy brown eyes. Midge gulped. She had never been this close to a waking human before. His face was enormous. Johnny yawned and Midge found herself staring into his wide open mouth. If those jaws snapped shut around her, she would be bitten clean in half. Hastily, she backed off to a safe distance.

"What are you?" asked Johnny.

Midge groaned as she realized she had managed to break all of the Three Abiding Rules in one go. She had looked in the box. She had not delivered what the customer ordered. And now she had been seen. Midge lifted her helmet up to her head and then let it drop again. It was too late for that. This human had already had a good look at her.

"Are you a fairy?" asked Johnny.

Midge scowled. *Fairy!* She hated that word. Dream Fetchers had been delivering dreams to humans for centuries. They always tried not to be seen, but, every now and then, it happened. Most human adults who spotted a Dream Fetcher thought they had seen a small bat or a very big insect. Human children were different. They always knew exactly what they had seen – and they weren't afraid to talk about it. Now there were hundreds of human stories about "fairies". Midge scowled even harder. She was not some silly, glittery creature with wings sprouting

out of her shoulders! She did not float about in a dress made from cobwebs and dew! And she definitely did not sleep in a buttercup!

"I'm not a fairy!" growled Midge. "I'm a—" She stopped herself from saying it just in time.

"A what? What are you?" asked Johnny, staring at her pointy ears and her tilted, almond-shaped eyes.

Midge thought about making a run for it, but she knew she had to sort out this mess somehow. Johnny was wide awake now – and he was starting to look frightened. Midge reached for the emergency sleeping powder canister that was clipped to her belt.

"All right, yes. I'm a – a –" Midge forced herself to spit out the word. "A fairy. And I've come to, um, do a magic spell."

Johnny's eyes widened. "Really?"

"Yes. But you mustn't tell anyone, or it won't work."

Johnny nodded. He looked at the tiny canister that Midge was pointing at him. "Is that your fairy wand?"

"Yes," said Midge, through gritted teeth. "That's my fairy wand. And the spell I'm going to do is for anyone starting a new school tomorrow."

"That's me," whispered Johnny, looking at his new school uniform.

"Yes, well. This is a 'My New School Will Be Brilliant' spell. That means tomorrow is going to be OK. OK…?"

Johnny's worried face relaxed into a smile. "OK," he said, sinking back into his pillows.

"Hold still while I spray— I mean, while I make the wish." Midge put on her helmet and zoomed towards

Johnny's head. She pressed the button on the canister. A fine mist of silvery dust drifted down onto Johnny's face. A second later he was fast asleep. Midge breathed a sigh of relief as she steered through the open window and out into the night.

As Midge soared up into the sky, she activated the dreamcom in her helmet. She might as well get this over with. "Midge to Dreamside," she said into her mouthpiece.

"Dreamside receiving you," said Team Leader Flint into her ear. "Make your report."

"Failed dream-drop," said Midge.

There was a silence. Midge held her breath.

"Failed?" asked Team Leader Flint suspiciously. "How?"

"I dropped it too soon," said Midge. "It

hit the floor instead of the human."

"My trainee Dream Fetchers do *not* fumble a basic *drop!*" yelled Team Leader Flint.

Midge winced as her earpiece squawked. "Sorry, boss. What now?" she asked.

There was another silence. Midge waited to hear her fate.

"Very well," said Team Leader Flint. "You will undertake twelve extra hours of dream-drop training. Understood?"

"Understood, boss."

"Return to base," growled Team Leader Flint.

Midge turned off her dreamcom with a sigh of relief. Flint was giving her a second chance! As Midge looked back at Johnny's lamp-lit window, she was glad she had broken the Three Abiding Rules. Now Johnny was expecting his new school to be brilliant. In the morning he was going to walk in through the school gates with his head up and a smile on his face – and that would make all the difference to his first day. As she headed back to Dreamside to face the anger of Team Leader Flint, Midge could not stop smiling.

Monsters

"**Whoo-hooo!**" yelled Harley as her dreamskoot shot through the dark Earthside tunnel. She looked over her shoulder. Two bright headlights lit up her face. A train was thundering through the tunnel behind her. It was very close. Harley grinned.

"OK," she said, patting the saddle of her dreamskoot. "Let's see how fast you can really go."

She twisted the handlebar throttle. The dreamskoot jumped forward. Harley flattened herself against the saddle. She steered through the tunnel, following the silver curves of the railway tracks. Behind her, the train was getting closer. Harley turned a corner and saw the end of the tunnel straight ahead.

"Time to climb!" she yelled, pulling up on the handlebars. The dreamskoot rose until it was speeding along just under the tunnel roof. Harley looked over her shoulder again. The train was nearly on top of her. Harley flew out of the end of the tunnel, centimetres ahead of it. "Up!" she ordered, hauling on the handlebars to help her dreamskoot along. The little machine shot straight up into the air. The train roared past below. A blast of air hit Harley and her dreamskoot, sending them tumbling up into the sky.

"Oh, yeah!" said Harley, as soon as she had her dreamskoot under control. "Let's do that again!"

She was about to dive back into the tunnel when Team Leader Flint spoke sharply into her earpiece. "Harley! Will you stop fooling around and get that dream delivered!"

"Yes, boss," said Harley. She sighed as she checked her map and pointed her dreamskoot towards the delivery address. As far as Harley was concerned, delivering the dream was the least interesting part of the whole business. Harley loved flying. And speed. And taking risks. She was told that she took after her mother. Harley hoped so: her mother had been a hero. Her father too. They had died in the infamous Battle of the Gateway when she was only a baby.

The Battle of the Gateway was an

event that would always be remembered in Dreamside. It had happened in one of the southern dream centres, just after a new gateway had been opened into an Earthside storm drain. After the disaster, every gateway was fitted with a fail-safe three-filter protection system, but in those days one filter had been thought to be enough. The gateway filter prevented Earthside molecules of any sort from passing through into Dreamside, but nobody realized that on that day the filter had stopped working. When a pack of vicious sewer rats came streaming through the gateway from the Earthside storm drain, the dream centre had been totally unprepared. Those inside the building, including Harley's mother and father, had bravely blocked all the exits and trapped the rats inside with them. What happened next was a

long and bloody battle. When the doors
were finally opened again, not a single
rat was left alive, but hundreds of dream
centre staff also lay dead, including
Harley's parents.

Harley's face grew sad for a moment,
and her ears drooped slightly inside her
helmet. She touched the tattered old
kerchief that she always wore, cowboy-
fashion, around her neck. It had once
belonged to her mother. Once again,
Harley wished she could have known her
mum and dad. But I have a new family

now, she thought, brightening. My dream team. Harley smiled as she remembered how Midge had fussed over her on the launch pad before take-off, straightening her uniform and warning her not to take too many risks. Vert had given her a quick hug and wished her luck. Snaffle had sneered as usual, but Harley was sure there was more to Snaffle than sneers.

Harley sighed. She was getting bored with this mission. When a small wood appeared on the horizon, she grinned. Quickly she zipped down into the wood and darted between the trunks of the trees as fast as she could.

"Harley," warned Team Leader Flint. "We can see you. You're making a zig-zag pattern on our monitor screens."

"Yes, boss," sighed Harley. This was no fun. She thought about turning off her tracker device so that Team Leader Flint could not follow her progress on the Control Tower screens, but decided against it. She had to pass her solo flying test if she wanted to become a Dream Fetcher. She was supposed to be delivering a dream to a boy called Daniel. He lived just on the other side of the wood. Harley flew out of the trees, towards Daniel's house. It was a mansion with a big garden and an ornamental fountain.

"Very fancy," Harley said to herself as she flew up to Daniel's window. It was firmly shut. So were all the other windows. Harley remembered what it said in her Dream Fetcher training book: "There is always a way in. You just have to find it."

"OK," muttered Harley, scanning the outside of the house. She spotted a large conservatory at one end. There was a fan set into the glass. It was turned off and the blades were still. Harley flew over and slipped through the gap between the blades of the fan.

Inside, she skimmed silently across a big swimming pool and then flew through a doorway into a grand entrance hall. The moon shone in through a high, arched window, lighting up a sweeping staircase.

Harley brought her dreamskoot to a

halt and pressed a button on the side of her helmet. A green eye glass slid into place on her visor. Harley peered at the hallway through the eye glass.

"Ha! Thought so," she said. "Security."

Through the eye glass, Harley could see a web of laser beams criss-crossing the hallway. They showed up as lines of red light. Humming to herself, she zig-zagged up the staircase, dodging laser beams all the way.

There were no beams on the upstairs landing. Harley pressed the button on her helmet and the eye glass folded away. Daniel's bedroom door was open and the room beyond was lit with a

flickering light. Harley eased her
dreamskoot through the doorway into
the bedroom.

Daniel was asleep in an enormous
bed, propped up on a pile of pillows.
Popcorn was scattered all over his duvet.

There was even a bit stuck on the end of his nose. An empty two-litre fizzy drink bottle lay beside him. The flickering light was coming from the screen of a home cinema system. Daniel had left a monster movie playing with the sound turned down.

Harley followed the Dream Fetcher drill and checked for other humans or Earth-pets. The big bedroom was packed full of things to keep Daniel happy. There was a pool table, a sofa, a chocolate machine, a mini-fridge and a popcorn maker. One wall was stacked high with computer games and music equipment. The rest of the wall space was covered with posters of vampires, dinosaurs, zombies and aliens. Another doorway led to Daniel's private bathroom. He had left the light on and a tap running. Harley yawned as she flew back into the bedroom. There were no waking humans or Earth-pets anywhere. This was going to be a safe, simple delivery.

"Boring," she muttered.

She pulled the dream box from the holder on the back of her dreamskoot. If she made a fast drop, she might have time to squeeze in some extra flying practice on the way back to base. She hovered above Daniel's head and looked down to make sure she was on target. The crumb of popcorn on the end of his nose was vibrating every time he snored. Harley looked at the popcorn and smiled. Perhaps this dream-drop could become a bit more exciting after all.

Harley narrowed her eyes. She was about to try a very tricky bit of flying. She was planning to zoom in on Daniel's face from the side, post the dream into his mouth and pluck the popcorn from the end of his nose, all in one smooth movement. It would need perfect timing. She would have to post the dream box and grab the popcorn at the same time. With both hands off the handlebars, she would have to steer her dreamskoot with her knees. Harley grinned. She could never resist a challenge.

"Here goes!" Harley flew down to the target zone, tilting her dreamskoot so that it came in at just the right angle. One hand held the dream box, the other held the handlebars steady. At the last second, Harley gripped her dreamskoot with her knees and let go of the handlebars. The dreamskoot stayed on course. Harley slid in neatly under Daniel's nose, catching a blast of hot air from his nostrils. She leant out over his mouth and pushed the dream box into the narrow gap between his lips. At the same time, her other hand was reaching out to pluck the popcorn from his nose …

Phut!

Harley never reached the popcorn. As soon as the dream touched Daniel it dissolved. Harley was still holding onto one corner of the box. Instantly, she felt a strange sensation spreading up her arm. She looked down. Her eyes widened in horror. Her arm was stretching out like a piece of chewing gum.

She was being sucked into the dream!
Harley tried to turn her dreamskoot
away, but she was too late. Down she
went, spinning into darkness.

When Harley woke up, she was no
longer in Daniel's bedroom. She was
lying on the cold stone floor of an old
castle. The high windows were shuttered
and the only light came from torches
burning in wall brackets. There was no
sign of her dreamskoot. Harley groaned.
She had been so busy trying to be clever

that she had forgotten one of the basic Dream Fetcher safety rules.

Always let go of the dream before it touches the human.

Harley had heard all the stories about Dream Fetchers who did not let go of the box in time. Being sucked into a human dream was very dangerous. Only a few Dream Fetchers managed to find a way out. Most were never seen again.

"Yeah, well, I'm not sticking around in someone else's dream," muttered Harley, clambering to her feet. "I'm getting out of here."

"You can't," said a soft voice.

Harley spun around. A human male was standing right behind her.

"Are you threatening me?" snapped Harley.

The human took a step back. "No, no, no!" he said in a flustered sort of a way.

"What I meant was, you can't do it on your own. I'm here to rescue you."

"Oh, really?" said Harley doubtfully. She inspected him carefully. He was tall and handsome, with thick fair hair and sparkling blue eyes. He was wearing a high-collared shirt, an old-fashioned silk tie, tight riding breeches and a long black cloak. There was a piece of popcorn stuck on the end of his nose.

"Yes, really. You see, I'm a hero," said the human, smugly. He made a sweeping bow. "At your service," he said. "My name is—"

"—Daniel!" said Harley, suddenly realizing what the popcorn meant.

"I'm not Daniel," said Daniel, sounding even more flustered. "My name is – um – Dirk Strong. And you're a lady who needs rescuing. See?"

Daniel turned Harley around and

pointed to a big, gold-framed mirror that had suddenly appeared on the wall. Harley looked at herself in the mirror and gave a small scream. The human staring back at her had long curly hair and shiny red lips. She was wearing a scarlet dress with a tight bodice and an enormous skirt that trailed along the ground behind her.

"I'm a human!" she gasped. "In a really silly dress!"

Suddenly, there was a loud creaking sound. The wooden door next to the mirror was swinging open.

"Don't worry," said Daniel, watching a very thin, very pale human walk through the doorway into the room. "I'll save you."

"Excuse me?" said Harley. She was not sure that she needed saving. The red-eyed human gliding towards them looked as

though a
strong breeze
would blow him
over. He was so
thin, he wasn't
even showing
up in the
mirror.

Daniel
ignored
Harley.
"Count
Dracula, I
presume?" he
said, reaching inside his cloak and
pulling out a wooden stake.

"Oh, I get it!" said Harley. "He's a
vampire!"

The vampire bared his long teeth.
Daniel raised his stake, getting ready to
plunge it through the vampire's heart.

"No need for all that messy business," said Harley, marching over to one of the windows. She yanked open the shutters and sunlight streamed into the castle. The vampire gave a surprised squeak and crumbled away into a little pile of dust.

"Easy-peasy!" said Harley. "Now all we need is a dustpan and brush." She turned to Daniel with a triumphant grin. Daniel was not smiling. He was scowling. "What?" said Harley.

"That's not supposed to happen," grumbled Daniel. "*I'm* supposed to rescue *you*."

Harley started to say something rude. She never got the chance to finish. Daniel, the castle and the pile of dust all faded away until only Daniel's scowl was left hanging in mid-air.

Harley rubbed her eyes.

When she
opened them
again, she was
standing in a
jungle clearing.
She looked down
at herself and
tutted with
annoyance. Now
she was wearing a
very short fur tunic

and a necklace made out of
animal bones.

"Oh, very practical," she sighed.

Something came crashing through the
jungle towards her. Harley grabbed a
fallen tree branch and prepared to
defend herself. The crashing sounds
came nearer. Harley could hear
something grunting as it slashed its
way through the undergrowth. She

swallowed and gripped her tree branch harder.

Suddenly, a whole curtain of creepers and vines fell to the jungle floor. Harley held her breath, waiting to see what would come out of the gap behind the creepers.

A dark, handsome human stepped into the clearing and slid his knife back into the sheath at his belt. He was wearing a sweat-stained safari hat, crumpled khakis and sturdy brown boots. His shirt was open to the waist and he had a bandolier of bullets slung across his hairy chest. There was a coiled bull whip on his shoulder – and a piece of popcorn stuck to his nose.

"Don't tell me," sighed Harley. "Let me guess. You've come to rescue me."

"Stop your screaming, sister," drawled Daniel. "Do you wanna bring the whole jungle down on us?"

"I wasn't screaming!" protested
Harley. "And I'm not your sister."

Daniel put a finger to his lips. "Shhh!"

Harley listened. Something else was
crashing through the jungle towards
them. Something much bigger than a
human. A terrible roar shook the treetops. The ground began to tremble.
Harley turned in a circle, trying to look
everywhere at once. The roar came
again, much closer now.

"What *is* that?" said Harley.

For answer, Daniel pointed at the
treetops just behind Harley. She turned.
A huge, scaly head was pushing up
through the leaves. The skull was flat,
with a long snout. The eyes were green
and gold, with black, slitted pupils. The
powerful jaws were open, showing two
rows of sharp fangs. Another roar

blasted down into the clearing and Harley staggered backwards.

"It's a dinosaur," she gasped.

"Tyrannosaurus Rex," said Daniel happily. He pulled the whip from his shoulder and stepped forward.

"Are you mad?" yelled Harley. "You can't beat a dinosaur by flicking a bit of leather at it!"

"I'm a hero, remember?" said Daniel, taking another step towards the dinosaur.

Harley groaned. It was all right for Daniel. Even if he got his head bitten off in his dream, he would still wake up safe in his own bed. She, on the other hand, was part of the dream. She would not survive a dinosaur attack. There had to be another way! Frantically, Harley tried to remember everything she had learned about dinosaurs in Earth History lessons.

"Oh!
Of course!"
said Harley.
"Hey! You
up there!"
Daniel
and the
Tyrannosaurus Rex
both turned to look at her.

"Not you! *You!* The one with the
oversized head and the silly little arms!
Everyone knows dinosaurs died out before
the first humans arrived. So, if he's here,
then you can't be, can you? You're an
impossibility!"

The dinosaur's
shoulders
slumped.
It looked
pleadingly at
Daniel.

"No use looking at him!" shouted Harley. "He can't change history!"

The dinosaur made a sorrowful little moan and hung its huge head.

"You're extinct," snapped Harley. "Skoot."

The dinosaur turned and shambled off through the trees, grumbling sadly to itself. Harley sighed with relief and then jumped as a whip cracked loudly. She turned to see Daniel glaring at her.

"That wasn't supposed to happen," growled Daniel.

Harley was astonished. "But – I just saved us."

"Well, don't! You're only supposed to scream and stuff. I do the saving!"

He was quivering with anger, and the popcorn on the end of his nose was trembling. Harley bit the insides of her cheeks to stop a smile.

"One more chance," snarled Daniel, turning his back on her.

"What do you mean?" demanded Harley, but Daniel and the jungle clearing were already fading away.

Harley blinked.

When she opened her eyes again, she was standing in a dark corridor. The steel walls were dripping with water. The floor was a metal grid. There were lights set into the low roof, but they were smashed and broken. A few still flickered on and off and bright fizzles of electrical sparks came from the others.

Harley looked down at herself in the flickering blue light. She was wearing army boots, combat trousers and a green vest. There was a rucksack on her back.

"What now, sir?" said a voice beside her.

Harley turned. A young human soldier was standing there. Five other soldiers were clustered around him. They all looked frightened.

"What now?" said a deep, rough voice on Harley's other side. "We move in and finish them off! That's what!"

Harley turned to see who was talking. A big, hard-looking human was glaring at the young soldier. His crew-cut hair bristled like pins. Muscles bulged out of his grubby vest. His chin was covered in stubble and he was chewing on a toothpick. There was a piece of popcorn stuck on the end of his nose.

The other humans nodded and turned to face the metal door in front of them. They all looked frightened. Harley wondered what was on the other side of the door.

"Sanchez!" snapped Daniel.

"Sir?" said the young soldier.

"Switch on your alien-tracker!"

Sanchez pointed a long tube at the door and then looked at the small screen that was strapped to his arm. Harley peered over his shoulder. The screen showed the corridor as lines of green light. It looked empty.

"No aliens, sir," said Sanchez.

Ping...

The alien-tracker blipped once. A single green blob appeared on the screen. Sanchez went pale.

Ping … ping … ping! Ping! Ping-ping-ping-ping-PING-PING!

"They're all around us, sir!" gasped Sanchez, staring at the green blobs that had suddenly invaded the screen.

"But where are they?" said another soldier, spinning to look behind him.

"They must be in the walls!" screamed Sanchez.

Harley reached out and smacked the side of the screen. The blips stopped. The green blobs all vanished.

"Thought so," she said. "Bad reception. A good thump usually sorts it out. There are no aliens here."

The soldiers all let out sighs of relief. Daniel scowled at Harley. "Let's just see, shall we?" He reached out and pressed a button on the wall. The door hissed open onto another corridor. It was empty.

"Yeah, well," said Daniel. "That's because they're – um – hiding from us! So let's go get 'em!"

The soldiers all started moving forward.

"Hang on a minute," said Harley.

Everybody stopped. Daniel turned to look at her with a warning glint in his eye. "What?"

"Why do we have to 'go get 'em'?"

"Pardon?"

"This is their planet, not ours. This is their home."

"So?"

"So why don't we just go back to our own planet and leave them alone?"

"Because they're aliens, stupid!" snarled Daniel. "Let's move in!"

But the other soldiers were muttering amongst themselves. Finally, Sanchez stepped forward. "Sir? We don't want to kill any more aliens. We want to go home."

"What!"

"We've had enough, sir. We're heading back to the spaceship."

"Mutiny!" snarled Daniel, chomping his toothpick in half as he watched his soldiers walk away. He turned on Harley. "I warned you! That was your last chance!"

Harley looked at Daniel. Something strange was happening. His chest swelled up until his dirty vest tore right in half. His bristly hair grew longer and turned into clawed tentacles. His mouth sprouted fangs and his nose turned into a tusk, still with the piece of popcorn balanced on its tip.

"Well, look at you," said Harley, folding her arms. "You turned out to be the biggest monster of them all."

The Daniel-monster roared and grabbed Harley in its tentacles. One of the claws ripped into the rucksack on her back. Harley tried to wriggle free, but she was caught fast.

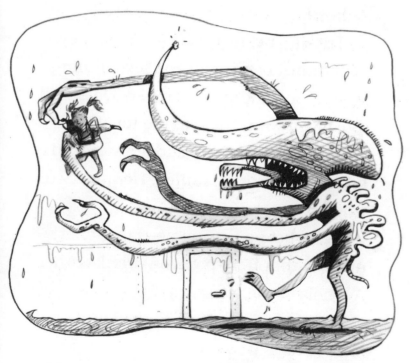

I have to break his dream, she thought, as the Daniel-monster pulled her towards its snarling mouth. But how? She looked around and saw the water dripping down the walls. Harley's eyes widened. She turned back to the Daniel-monster.

"Can you hear that water, Daniel?"

The Daniel-monster stopped and tilted its head.

"Trickle, trickle, trickle," said Harley. "That must be the tap you left running in your bathroom, remember? Doesn't it make you want to go to the toilet?"

The Daniel-monster suddenly looked a bit worried. Harley smiled. Her plan was working.

"Yes, I bet you really need the toilet after all that fizzy pop you drank earlier. A whole bottle, wasn't it?"

The Daniel-monster groaned and crossed its legs.

"Don't you think you'd better wake up, before you *wet the bed!*"

The Daniel-monster squawked and dropped Harley. She closed her eyes and waited to hit the metal floor of the corridor. Instead she landed on something soft and bouncy and then shot up into the air again. She opened her eyes. She was on her dreamskoot, hovering above Daniel's empty bed. She had survived the dream!

"Up!" snapped Harley. She wanted to get out of sight as quickly as possible. Her dreamskoot rose up towards the ceiling. Harley scanned the room and spotted Daniel. He was halfway across the floor, hobbling towards his bathroom as fast as he could go with his legs crossed. Harley grinned. She had not been seen.

Harley checked herself over. Her mother's tattered old kerchief was back around her neck. Harley patted it affectionately and then straightened her uniform jacket. Something sharp dug into her spine. Harley reached around behind her. A large claw was hooked into the back of her jacket. Harley prised the claw loose. "That was close," she muttered, opening her dream-holder and wedging the claw inside. "Perhaps I should start being more careful."

She tried it. Turning her dreamskoot, she glided slowly and carefully to the door.

"Boring!" she grinned.

Harley leant over her saddle and opened up the throttle. A few minutes later, a small silver streak blasted out of the swimming-pool fan, did a loop-the-loop around the ornamental fountain and shot off into the sky.

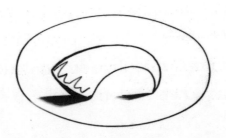

The Dancing Dream

Vert was terrified. He was trembling so much that all the zip fasteners on his uniform were jingling. He eyed his dreamskoot, trying to find the courage to climb aboard. Midge and Harley had both made their first solo flights. Now it was Vert's turn.

Team Leader Flint spoke into his dreamcom. "Vert?"

Vert looked up at the Control Tower windows. Team Leader Flint was looking down at him. Her face was serious.

"Are you ready?"

Vert nodded, but stayed where he was. The truth was, he was not at all ready. The truth was, he wanted to turn around and run away from his dreamskoot as fast as he could. He was sweating so much, his helmet was misting up. Vert lifted the visor and wiped his face. He looked over at the other three members of his dream team. Midge smiled encouragingly. Harley gave him a thumbs-up. Snaffle sneered.

"Vert. The dream is getting cold," warned Team Leader Flint.

Vert looked at the flat cardboard box in the padded carrier on the back of his dreamskoot. The order was for a human girl called Melissa Plumb. He had recognized her name as soon as it came up on the screen and had only just managed to keep his face blank. The thing was, Vert knew what was in the box. He had not exactly lied to Team Leader Flint earlier that morning. It was true that he had not seen any dreams being made that day. But he had caught a glimpse of Melissa's completed dream. Motza, the Head Dream Chef, had been showing it off to the other chefs just before it went into the box. It was a beautiful dream – a work of art. Vert sighed. He could not let such a beautiful dream go to waste. Taking a deep

breath, he sprinted up to his dreamskoot,
flung himself into the saddle, overshot
and fell off the other side.

"Whumphhh!" he gasped as he landed
on his back on the launch-pad floor.
Everything went blurry. Vert closed his
eyes. When he opened them again, three
faces were looking down at him.

"That was very funny," sniggered
Snaffle. "Do it again."

"Shut up, Snaffle," said Harley,
grabbing Vert by the arm.

"Up you come, Vert!" grinned Midge,

grabbing his other arm.

Midge and Harley pulled Vert to his feet and brushed him down.

"Slowly does it," said Team Leader Flint into his earpiece. "No need to rush. Your dreamskoot won't go anywhere until you say so."

Vert eased himself back onto his dreamskoot. This time he managed to stay in the saddle. He pulled down his helmet visor and the dreamskoot wobbled beneath him. Vert lunged forward and grabbed the handlebars as tightly as he could. He heard Snaffle laugh.

"Vert," said Team Leader Flint. "Look at me."

Vert kept his head perfectly still and rolled his eyes to the side like a frightened pony. All he could see was the inside of his helmet.

"Vert. Turn your head and look at me."

Vert turned his head very slowly until he could see his boss standing at the windows of the Control Tower. Team Leader Flint cupped her hand around her mouthpiece so that nobody in the Control Tower could hear what she had to say.

"Listen carefully, Vert. Do you want to stop? You can, you know. If you want to stop, just nod."

Vert gazed up at Team Leader Flint. He wanted to nod so badly, but his mum and dad were up in the Control Tower too. They had been given special permission to come and watch their son make his first solo flight. They were standing at the window, side by side, dressed in their best clothes. They looked so proud.

Vert took another deep breath and

gabbled out the four steps of the launch procedure before he could change his mind. "Power up! Lift off! Wings out! Earthside!"

His dreamskoot left the launch pad and shot towards the gateway in the far wall of the Dream Centre. All around him, other dreamskoots were zipping past. Vert knew that each dreamskoot heading in or out of the gateway was on autopilot and every flight path was carefully plotted by the Dream Traffic Controllers. There had never been a crash, but still Vert winced every time another dreamskoot cut across his bows.

Vert closed his eyes as his dreamskoot flew into the huge round gateway. For a few seconds the dreamskoot slowed, and Vert had the feeling of being dragged through warm jelly. Then, suddenly the jelly was gone. Instead, Vert felt cold air rushing over him. He had passed through to Earthside. Now he could no longer rely on the autopilot to fly his dreamskoot. He had to take over the controls. Unfortunately, in order to do that he had to open his eyes.

Vert groaned. He had scraped through all the training flights by sticking to Team Leader Flint like glue. He had discovered that if he followed the tail-lights of her dreamskoot and did not look down, he could keep his fear under control. After every flight, Flint had stared into Vert's green, sweaty face and asked if there was anything he wanted to tell her. Vert had always shaken his head. His mum and dad were so proud that their son was going to be a Dream Fetcher. He did not have the heart to let them down.

Which was how he had ended up here,

flying solo with his eyes shut. Vert forced one eye open. This time there were no comforting tail-lights to follow. He was on his own with the whole of the night sky spread out around him. His head began to whirl. His stomach tried to turn itself inside out. Vert gasped and squeezed his eye shut again. He lunged forward and wrapped his arms around the handlebars. Bad mistake. With no one to steer it, his dreamskoot dipped forward and went into a dive.

Blip! Blip! Blip!

An alarm began to sound on his control panel. His dreamskoot was losing height too fast. Vert whimpered and tried to bury his head in the saddle.

Beep! Beep! Beep!

Another alarm rang out in competition with the first one. Vert gave a strangled scream. His D.R.E.A.M.'s early warning system had been activated. The D.R.E.A.M. was a radar device fitted to the front of his dreamskoot. The letters stood for Danger Recognition and Early Avoidance Monitor. The early warning alarm meant only one thing. A large, solid object was dangerously close. Vert was guessing that, in his case, the large, solid object was probably the ground.

Vert was frozen with fear. All he could do was cling on to his dreamskoot as it plummeted towards Earth with all its warning lights flashing.

"Lights!" croaked Vert. "That's the answer!" He

opened his eyes and lifted his head just high enough to see the dashboard in front of him. There were two brightly lit screens on the control panel. One was a street map of the Earthtown below. The other green-lit screen showed a network of circles and lines that looked like a target. This screen was connected to the D.R.E.A.M. In theory, Vert could steer his dreamskoot without having to look anywhere except at the two screens right in front of him. It would be just like following Team Leader Flint's tail-lights.

Keeping his eyes firmly on the two screens, Vert sat up. He grabbed the handlebars and started to pull the dreamskoot out of its dive. The little machine whined and shuddered and then finally levelled out just in time to avoid crashing through the Town Hall roof. It scraped and bumped along the slates then slid off the guttering and shot off down the High Street. Vert took a very shaky breath. His first solo flight had nearly been his last.

By the time he reached the building where his customer lived, Vert was a nervous wreck. It had been easy enough to find his way using the on-screen map, but his D.R.E.A.M. screen had been much harder to use. It only showed approaching obstacles as shapeless green blobs. Vert was too scared to look up from the screen, so he had no idea what he was heading for until it was right in front of him. He had narrowly missed crashing into a tall chimney, a water tower and a statue of a human on a horse.

"Never mind," he told himself, peering at his control panel. "I'm here now. The delivery address should be right ahead—"

Vert's voice dried up. He stared in horror at the enormous green blob that was taking up the whole of his D.R.E.A.M. screen.

"Brake!" he screamed.

His dreamskoot stopped so suddenly that it tipped up onto its nose before settling down to hover just above the pavement. Vert raised his head to see what was blocking his way to the delivery address.

"Oh, no," he breathed.

The huge obstacle on his D.R.E.A.M. screen *was* the delivery address. Vert was looking at a high-rise block of flats. He gulped and peered at the map screen for delivery details.

"Melissa Plumb. Top floor…"

Vert tilted his head back as far as it would go. The building was so high that he could not see the top. His stomach tried to turn inside out again. For an awful moment, Vert thought he was going to be sick into his helmet. Then he thought of the beautifully baked dream on the back of his dreamskoot.

"I'm not giving up now!" he snapped, grabbing the handlebars. "Straight up!"

The dreamskoot did just what he ordered. Vert clung on as it skooted up the side of the huge building. "It's a road," he said, staring at the vertical wall skimming past below his feet. "It's a very flat road."

Finally, the dreamskoot reached the top floor. Vert counted along the line of windows until he reached Melissa's bedroom. Her window was shut, but the little bathroom window beside it was open. He steered his dreamskoot inside.

The flat was dark and quiet. He flew out into the hallway. Melissa's bedroom door was open and a soft light was seeping out. Vert lifted his visor. His heart was beating so fast, it sounded like thunder in his ears. "Here goes," he muttered, heading into the room.

Melissa was asleep. Vert did a quick check for other humans and pets. The room was clear. He brought his dreamskoot in to land on Melissa's bedside table. Vert gave the solid wood beneath him an affectionate glance and saw that he had landed on a piece of paper.

Ballet Exam, it said at the top of the page. Vert read on. *Melissa Plumb, Grade Two. Your exam will start at ten o'clock. Please be warmed up and ready.*

Vert nodded. Melissa had ordered a dancing dream and now he understood why. She was worried about doing well in her ballet exam the next morning. Vert smiled as he pulled the flat cardboard box from the holder. He knew the dream would make her feel better. In this dream, Melissa would dance like an angel.

Vert gripped the box in one hand and took off. He hovered over the bed and let the dream go.

Perfect drop! he thought as the box headed straight for Melissa. Then something shot out from under the bed. It jumped up and lunged for him. Vert saw bristling fur and snarling jaws. A dog! The dream box disappeared into the dog's mouth.

Vert had a nightmare glimpse of glistening teeth and a red, slavering

tongue. He yanked his dreamskoot to the
right. He heard the dog's jaws snap shut
a whisker away from him. Vert and his
dreamskoot tumbled through the air,
bounced off the duvet and headed for
the floor. *Why didn't I check under the
bed?* he thought as he clung to the
handlebars and waited for the impact.

Whumph! He landed softly in a pile of
screwed-up clothes. Vert said a quick

thank you to Melissa for being so untidy. But now he had another problem. His dreamskoot was stuck inside a small pink ballet shoe. Vert opened the throttle. "Reverse!" he ordered.

The dreamskoot whined, but its nose was wedged into the toe of the ballet shoe. Vert heard a growl. He looked up. The dog was standing in the middle of the floor with its lips curled back into a snarl.

"Reverse!" squeaked Vert.

This time the dreamskoot shifted a little, but the dog had started to move. It was stalking across the carpet towards him.

"Bad dog!" shouted Vert. "Down! Sit!"

The dog growled and kept on coming.

"Reverse!" screamed Vert.

The dreamskoot shot backwards out of the shoe and got stuck in the tangle of ribbons that were sewn to the heel.

Vert groaned. The dog crouched down on its haunches. It was getting ready to attack. Vert closed his eyes and waited to be swallowed. Nothing happened. Vert opened his eyes again. He stared at the dog in disbelief. Something strange had happened to it. The glaring eyes had become soft and dreamy. The snarling jaws were now pouting prettily.

"What...?" said Vert.

The dog fluttered its eyelashes at Vert and rose up onto its hind legs. It lifted its front legs above its head and pointed its claws. Then the dog began to dance. It twirled across the floor, tilting its head this way and that. It went up on one hind paw and stuck the other one out behind it.

"The dream!" breathed Vert. "The dog is having the dream!"

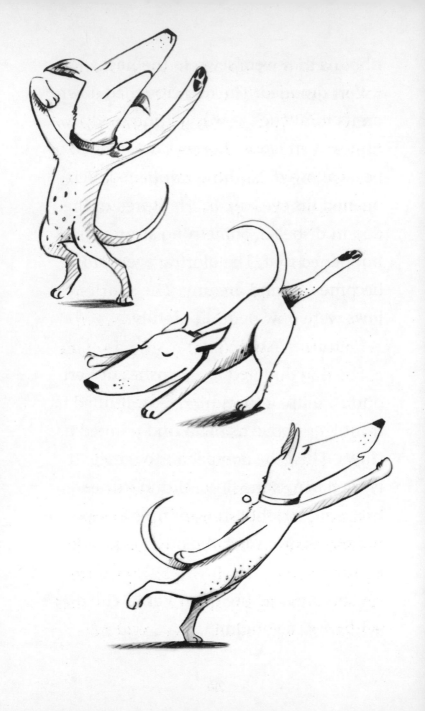

The dog went up on its tippy-toes and tottered across the carpet. It took no notice of Vert as he freed his dreamskoot from the ribbons. Vert rose into the air and looked down. Now the dog was pushing its back paws into Melissa's pink ballet shoes. Vert turned to look at Melissa. She was still asleep with an anxious little frown on her face, waiting for her dream to arrive. Vert groaned. What a mess! Vert did the only thing he could think of. He fled.

Back at the Dream Centre, Vert escaped from all the hugs and congratulations as soon as he could. Only he knew that his dream delivery had not reached its target. Vert hurried to hide away in the place where he felt most at home. The dream kitchens. He stood quietly in a corner as Dream Chefs worked all around him. He could not forget the anxious frown on Melissa's face. Vert sighed, picked up a brush and started to sweep the floor. The chefs had dropped bits and pieces of dream toppings all over the kitchens. He might as well try to do one useful thing tonight.

"Vert!" called the Head Dream Chef, hurrying across the kitchen towards him. "She like my dream, your customer? I make it myself. Special for you. For your first delivery."

Vert looked up into the Head Chef's beaming face. "It was a beautiful dream," he stammered. "Thank you, Signore Mozzarella."

"Please, you call me Motza," said the Head Chef.

"Mozzarella – it is a bit, how you say...?"

"Girly?" suggested Vert.

Motza scowled thunderously. "Girly?"

"Yes. No! Well, just the '-ella' bit on the end," gabbled Vert. "Oh dear. I'm sorry, Motza, I didn't mean to—"

Motza threw back his head and laughed. "I joke! I tease, yes?"

Vert smiled weakly. "Oh. Ha, ha."

"You are a good boy, Vert," said Motza. "If you change your mind about fetching the dreams, you come here to me, OK? You work for me."

Vert hung his head to hide the tears in his eyes. If only Motza knew how much he wanted to be a Dream Chef! Motza patted Vert on the shoulder and bustled off. Vert blinked the tears away and looked down at the small pile of dream toppings at his feet. His eyes widened as an idea came to him.

"I can make another dancing dream!" he said to himself.

Vert hurried around the kitchen, gathering up bits of unbaked dream dough. He squashed them together and rolled the dough out into a flat circle. Some of the toppings were more difficult to find. Golden Grace in particular was rare and quite expensive, but finally he found a small slice lying forgotten at the back of a cupboard.

"In you go," whispered Vert, putting the dream onto a wooden paddle and sliding it to the back of a spare oven. Five minutes later, it was done. He sprinkled on some grated dream music

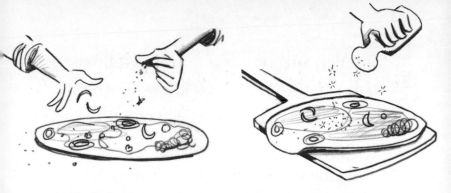

and slid the dream into a box.

Vert hurried out of the kitchens and stood at the back of the launch pad area. How was he going to get this dream to Melissa? He saw that Snaffle was mounted on his dreamskoot, getting ready to launch into his first solo flight. Vert hesitated. Would Snaffle take Melissa's dream for him? Vert took a step towards Snaffle's launch pad.

"Don't," said a voice, close to his ear.

Vert jumped. He looked around. Harley was standing beside him. "Don't what?" said Vert, trying to sound casual.

"Don't ask Snaffle to deliver it for you," said Harley, nodding down at the dream box Vert was holding. "Snaffle will tell Team Leader Flint. You know he will."

Vert sighed and looked down at the dream box. Harley was right.

"Come on, kiddo," said Harley. "Let's go and wave him off."

Vert hid his dream box behind his back and followed Harley out onto Snaffle's launch pad. Midge hurried out of the dreamskoot garages to join them.

"Good luck, Snaffle," they chorused as his dreamskoot powered up.

Snaffle turned with the beginnings of a smile on his face. When he saw that it was them, the smile turned into a sneer. "I don't need luck," sneered Snaffle, giving them a withering look. He turned to check his control panel, then looked back again at Vert, Harley and Midge. He glared at them for a few seconds, his face twisted into a ferocious scowl. Then he flipped down his helmet visor and took off.

"We love you too, Snaffle," muttered Midge, heading back to the dreamskoot garage.

"Now what am I going to do?" asked Vert, watching Snaffle shoot towards the gateway. "I have to get this dream to Melissa."

Harley glanced up at the Control Tower. Team Leader Flint had moved away from the windows to track Snaffle's journey on the monitor screens. "I'll take you," said Harley, turning back to Vert.

Vert stared at Harley. "You can't! You've done your solo flight already."

"I'll fly without instruments," said Harley. That way we won't be tracked by the Control Tower. We'll be invisible."

"Without instruments?" squeaked Vert. "Isn't that dangerous?"

Harley grinned. "Yeah! But I've done it

loads of times. How do you think I got to be so good at flying? Come on."

In a daze, Vert followed Harley out onto her launch pad.

"Won't somebody spot us?" he whispered, gazing around the huge, brightly lit Dream Centre as Harley climbed onto her dreamskoot.

"Not if you act as though you're supposed to be here," said Harley confidently. "They're all too busy to notice one more dreamskoot taking off."

Vert nodded and opened the padded holder on the back of Harley's dreamskoot. He tried to slip the dream box inside but something was already wedged in the holder. It looked like a large claw. "What's this?" asked Vert.

"Long story," grinned Harley, pulling the claw out of the holder and dropping it down the waste chute at the side of the launch pad. "Hop on, kiddo."

All dreamskoots were built to carry two. The saddle was long enough for Vert to fit snugly behind Harley. He wrapped his arms around her waist and hung on, grateful that someone else would be doing the flying this time.

Once they were Earthside, Harley flew at breakneck speed, diving and soaring and even looping-the-loop around the statue of the human on a horse. Vert kept his eyes shut the whole way and concentrated on not being sick into his helmet. He could hardly believe it when

they arrived at Melissa's flat in one piece.

Harley flew into Melissa's bedroom, keeping high above the floor in case the dog was still around. Vert gave a sigh of relief when he spotted the dog lying flat on its back in the middle of Melissa's ballet clothes. It was still wearing the little pink ballet shoes and had also managed to pull Melissa's tutu over its head. The pink netting of the tutu quivered every time the dog snored.

Vert grinned. He would love to see the look on the dog's face when it woke up again. Harley flew over to Melissa's bed and hovered there.

"Go, Vert," she whispered.

Vert made his dream-drop successfully this time. He nodded proudly as he watched the frown disappear from Melissa's face. She began to hum softly in her sleep. Her fingers twitched in time to the music. Vert's dancing dream had worked.

When Harley blasted back through the gateway into the Dream Centre, Vert had his eyes closed again. He did not notice that the whole centre was full of frantic activity.

"Oops," said Harley as she steered her dreamskoot down towards the launch pads, dodging back and forth to avoid all the other dreamskoots. "Looks like we may have been missed after all."

"What do you mean?" asked Vert, opening his eyes as Harley landed her dreamskoot neatly on the launch pad.

"Look over there," said Harley, pointing at the emergency launch pads. The Search and Rescue Dreamsquad were on their dreamskoots, preparing to launch.

"Oh no! We're in trouble now!" Vert

scrambled from Harley's dreamskoot and tottered onto the launch-pad walkway. Cheroot, the Head of Search and Rescue, was striding towards him. His face was as hard as stone and he was chewing on an unlit cigar. Vert felt his skin turn to ice.

"Um, excuse me?" he squeaked, stepping in front of Cheroot. "You can call off the search. I'm back."

"Out of my way, son," said Cheroot, pushing right past him.

"But it's me! I'm here!" called Vert, hurrying after Cheroot. "And Harley too…"

Cheroot waved him away as though he were an irritating insect.

"What's going on?" asked Harley, coming to stand beside Vert.

"I'm not sure," said Vert as other hurrying figures pushed past, taking no notice of them at all. "But whatever the panic is, we're not the cause of it."

"Aren't they wonderful?" sighed Harley, watching Cheroot and the Search and Rescue team prepare to go Earthside. "They're all volunteers, you know. They do this in their time off. I'm going to join them one day."

"Where have you two been?" said Midge, hurrying up to them. "I've been looking all over for you."

"Well," began Vert.

"Never mind," interrupted Midge. "I've found you now. Come on."

"Where are we going?" panted Vert

as he trotted along beside Midge, with
Harley striding after them.

"Up to the Control Room," said Midge,
grimly. "To watch the search."

"Who's missing?" asked Harley.

Midge stopped and pointed to Snaffle's
launch pad. It was empty. "Snaffle!"
gasped Vert. His chin quivered as he
looked at the empty launch pad. Snaffle
might be a pain, but he was still the
fourth member of their dream team.

"Yes, Snaffle," said Midge. "We've lost
contact with him. Snaffle has gone
missing on his first solo flight."

Missing in Action

Snaffle peered at the windows of the dreamskoot garage behind his launch pad. He was checking out his reflection in the glass. He smirked. He was pleased with what he saw. His trainee Dream Fetcher uniform had been made to measure by the best tailor in

Dreamside. It fitted perfectly and the shoulder pads made his chest look broader.

"Looking good," said Snaffle to his reflection.

He had also smartened up his dreamskoot in preparation for his first solo flight. The little machine now had a furry saddle cover and some go-faster stripes. He had even given his dreamskoot a name. Snaffle smiled proudly as he looked at the slanted gold lettering on the engine casing.

Speed Steed.

Harley had laughed at the name. She had tried to turn the laugh into a cough, but Snaffle had not been fooled. Now, as he sneered across at Harley's dreamskoot, Snaffle decided that Harley had laughed because she was jealous. Harley's dreamskoot had to be the scruffiest in the whole Dream Centre. She never polished it. Instead she spent all her spare time tinkering with the engine and oiling the wings.

"Ready for your solo flight, Snaffle?" asked Team Leader Flint into his dreamcom.

"Yes, boss," said Snaffle, snapping to attention and sending a smart salute in the direction of the Dream Traffic Control Tower. Team Leader Flint was standing at one of the windows. Snaffle checked the other windows, but there was no one else looking down at him. He took a quick look around the rest of the Dream Centre, checking the public viewing platform and the launch pad walkways.

"Are you expecting your family to be here?" asked Team Leader Flint.

"No, no! No, of course not. Not at all,"

said Snaffle, slamming down his helmet visor and climbing onto his dream-skoot. Only babies like Vert asked their mums and dads to come to their first solo flight. Snaffle was no baby. And a first solo flight was no big deal. Besides, his mother and father were both Area Commanders. Their jobs were much too important to take time off for such a little thing. Snaffle sat up straight in his saddle and his face was full of determination as he waited for his dream delivery to be brought out from the kitchens. This was going to be a faultless flight.

"Power up!" he commanded as soon as the dream was loaded onto his dreamskoot.

"Good luck, Snaffle!"

Snaffle's eyes widened with surprise and pleasure. His family had made it

after all! He twisted in his saddle, ready
to give them a casual wave, but there
was no sign of his mum and dad.
Instead Midge, Vert and Harley were
standing in a row on the walkway
behind his launch pad. Snaffle hid his
disappointment with a sneer. Midge,
Vert and Harley smiled back
encouragingly. "I don't need luck," said
Snaffle, turning his back on them.

Snaffle checked his control panel
– and felt his stomach turn over.
Something was wrong. Snaffle stared at

the power indicator. It was showing a very low power reading. Snaffle could not understand it. He had plugged a power cell into his dreamskoot. Everything should be fully charged.

Snaffle reached down and flipped open the cover of his dreamskoot's cell holder. The slot was empty. Had the power cell fallen out? He checked the floor of the launch pad. Nothing. There was only one explanation. Someone had taken the power cell in order to sabotage his first solo flight – and Snaffle had a pretty good idea who that was.

He turned to glare at Midge, Vert and Harley. They smiled back at him. Snaffle was furious. They were pretending they had come to wave him off but really they were waiting to see him abandon his solo flight test. Well, he would show them!

Snaffle turned back to his control

panel. He looked at his on-screen map and did some quick sums in his head. If he flew fast and straight, there was just a chance he might make it to the delivery address and back before his power ran out. But it was a very small chance and a very big risk. Snaffle hesitated. He thought about abandoning the flight. But then he thought about Midge, Vert and Harley. Snaffle's face twisted into a scowl.

"Lift off! Wings out! Earthside!" he snarled before he could change his mind.

His pride kept him going until he was through the gateway. It was only when the cold Earthside air hit him that Snaffle began to worry. Suddenly, he felt very small and very alone. He looked down at the Earthtown below. He looked back at the gateway. It was well hidden inside a pile of stones on the very top of the hill that overlooked the town, but Snaffle knew where to look. He could see it glowing softly in the moonlight. He gazed longingly at the gateway for a moment, but then he turned his dreamskoot around and shot off towards the town as fast as he could go.

Snaffle reached the delivery address in record time, but his power readings were dangerously low. He was delivering a simple, milky dream to a baby human. He knew it was a baby dream because they were always packed in special boxes to make sure there was never a mix-up. Babies could not cope with the highly spiced dreams that older humans sometimes ordered.

He peered in through the nursery window and groaned. The baby was fast asleep – but it was cradled in the arms of

a mother human. Dream Fetcher
procedure was simple in situations like
this. He was supposed to wait until the
mother human fell asleep or left the
room. Snaffle looked at his power gauge.
It was nearly down to the red danger

mark. He did not have time to wait.

Snaffle put his head down, shot in through the open window and headed for the baby.

"Oh!" screamed the mother human. "Oh! Help!"

The mother human flapped an arm at Snaffle. He dived under the arm, yanked the dream from the holder and threw it at the baby. It landed right on target. Snaffle zoomed out of range of the flapping arm and started heading back to the window, but then another human staggered into the room, cutting off Snaffle's escape route. It was the father human.

"What on earth...?" rumbled the father human, rubbing his face with one hand and holding up his pyjama bottoms with the other.

"It's a moth!" shrieked the mother

human. "A giant moth! Squish it! Squash it!"

Snaffle shot up to the ceiling and hovered there, panting with fear. But the father human did not try to squish him. The father human did not even look up.

"Only a moth?" sighed the father human. "You woke me up because of a moth?"

"A *giant* moth! Squish it! Squash it! I hate moths!"

"Shh! You'll wake the baby."

"Don't you shush me!" hissed the mother human, forgetting all about Snaffle. "I've been up every night this week while you lie there snoring!"

"I'm the one who has to get up for work in the mornings!" said the father human as Snaffle eased his way past.

"Oh! So you think I don't work?" said the mother human as Snaffle flew up to the top part of the bedroom window.

"I didn't say that," said the father human, hurrying towards the mother human as she started to cry.

Snaffle slipped through the opening and out into the street with a sigh of relief. He had not been squashed. But now he had another problem. His power gauge was flashing red. There was no way he could make it back to the gateway. Unless...

First, Snaffle turned off his lights. Then he turned off his saddle heater. His on-screen map was the next thing to go. Then he flicked off his dreamcom. Finally, Snaffle reached out and turned off his D.R.E.A.M. screen. Now the only lights showing on his control panel were his dreamskoot's tracker device and his power gauge. Snaffle peered at the gauge. It had risen just above the red.

He had enough power to limp home, but, with his Danger Recognition and Early Avoidance Monitor out of action, he would have to fly blind.

Snaffle set off. He had a pretty good idea of the way back. He crossed the park and then glided down the hill towards the town centre, turning off his engine to save power. Once he reached the High Street, Snaffle planned to fly up to the rooftops and head straight for the Town Hall clock. From there, if he set a course towards the Pole Star he would find his way back to the gateway on the hilltop. As long as his power lasted out.

He had nearly reached the bottom of the hill. A large supermarket loomed dead ahead. Snaffle knew the High Street was on the other side of the supermarket. He switched the power on again, rose up the side of the building and began to steer around a large flag that was flapping from the supermarket roof.

Snaffle was nearly past the flag, when suddenly it snapped in the wind and swung round to the other side of the flagpole. The flag wrapped around Snaffle and his dreamskoot, trapping them inside folds of rough canvas. Snaffle panicked. He turned the throttle up to full power and his dreamskoot

whined like a trapped bee. The canvas flapped around him like thunder and then snapped out straight again, flicking him off.

The dreamskoot tumbled over and over. All Snaffle could do was cling on and wait for the spinning to stop. Finally, his dreamskoot levelled out. Dizzily, Snaffle lifted his head and peered out through his visor. The dreamskoot was heading straight for a low concrete wall that edged the flat roof.

"Brake!" he screamed. The dreamskoot shuddered to a halt with centimetres to spare. Snaffle flopped over the handlebars, weak with relief. His dreamskoot engine coughed and spluttered. Snaffle sat up and looked at his power gauge. It was on empty. His struggles with the flag had drained the last of the power. The tracker light on his control panel flickered off. Slowly, his dreamskoot floated down and landed on the flat roof of the supermarket. The wings folded away. The engine gave one last cough and stopped.

"All right," breathed Snaffle, looking around the quiet rooftop. "No need to panic. Dream Traffic Control has this rooftop as my last known position. I just have to wait for them to come and get me."

Snaffle sat back to wait for the Search and Rescue team. A second later, a silent nightmare of feathers and claws fell out of the sky on top of him.

"What do you mean you can't find Snaffle!" roared Team Leader Flint. "You're supposed to be tracking him!"

The Dream Traffic Controller pointed a shaking finger at the red flashing light

on his monitor screen. "H-he was right there. Then he just disappeared. His tracker device has stopped working."

Flint stared at the flashing light for a few seconds and then turned and marched towards the screen on the back wall of the Control Tower. The Dream Traffic Controller scurried after her.

"Map!" yelled Flint.

A street map appeared on the

enormous screen. A red flashing dot marked Snaffle's last known position.

"Pinpoint!" ordered Flint.

The screen zoomed in on a small section of the map with the flashing red light at its centre.

"That's the supermarket just off the High Street," said the Dream Traffic Controller. "Snaffle must be up on the roof."

Flint clicked on her dreamcom. "Base to Snaffle," she said into her mouthpiece. "Come in, please."

There was no answer. Flint tried again.

"Base to Snaffle. Come in, please."

Silence. Flint tried a third time.

"Snaffle. This is Flint. Can you hear me? Are you lost? Are you – hurt?" She pressed the earpiece to her ear, straining to listen. There was no answer.

Flint strode across to a wall-mounted

alarm button and slammed the palm of
her hand against it. Immediately a siren
went off in the Search and Rescue area
and the team began scrambling for their
launch pads.

"Hang on, Snaffle," whispered Flint,
gazing up at the flashing light on the
map. "We're coming to get you."

Midge, Vert and Harley came in and
stood quietly in a corner of the Dream
Traffic Control Tower. Everyone was
watching the big screen. Six green dots

were speeding towards the red dot that marked Snaffle's last known position. Team Leader Flint paced back and forth as she watched. Every few seconds she tried to reach Snaffle on her dreamcom. There was no reply.

The six green dots on the screen reached the red dot. Everyone in the Control Tower held their breath. Finally, Cheroot's voice came over the loudspeakers. "We've reached the supermarket roof. Snaffle is not here. Repeat. Snaffle has disappeared."

Snaffle could hardly breathe. He was bent double over the saddle of his dreamskoot with his arms pinned underneath him. Just when he'd thought things could not get any worse, a huge owl had swooped down onto the supermarket roof and grabbed both him and his dreamskoot.

Now the owl was flying through the
night, with Snaffle and his dreamskoot
held in its talons. His face was squashed
against his helmet visor, and something
in the pocket of his uniform was digging
into his chest. It was square, with two
sharp prongs. Suddenly Snaffle groaned.
He had just realized that Midge, Vert
and Harley had not taken the power cell
from his dreamskoot. He had forgotten
to plug it in. The power cell was still in
his pocket. Snaffle had only himself to
blame for this mess.

He struggled to sit up, but the owl simply tightened its grip, crushing him further down into the saddle. He decided it would be safer to lie still. At least none of the needle-sharp talons had hurt him. They were all hooked under his saddle, trapping him inside a cramped, living cage.

His heart was beating fast. He could not see where the owl was taking him, but he knew that it must be further and further away from the supermarket roof. Snaffle groaned. How would Cheroot and the Search and Rescue team find him now?

The owl swerved downwards and flew into a dark, echoing place. It brought its talons out in front and started to beat its wings to slow down. A second later, the owl opened its talons and let Snaffle drop. Snaffle clung to his dreamskoot,

and they fell together into a smelly pile
of feathers and owl pellets. He could see
mouse bones and bits of fur in the
pellets. Snaffle scrambled off his
dreamskoot and struggled to his feet.
He was not going to let this owl eat *him*
without a fight! But the owl was flapping
away again. Snaffle watched it fly out of
a round opening in a stone wall. Snaffle
looked around. He was on a wide rafter,
high up in a church tower.

Snaffle heard a rustling behind him. He
turned around. He had been dropped into
a nest with two baby owls. They looked
very hungry. Snaffle dived behind his
dreamskoot and burrowed into the smelly
pile of feathers until only his helmet
visor was showing. The baby owls began
attacking his dreamskoot with their sharp
beaks. One ripped the furry cover from
the saddle. The other tried to grab it.

While the baby owls had a tug-of-war over the saddle cover, Snaffle pulled the power cell from his pocket and crept over to his dreamskoot. Keeping his head low, he pushed the power cell into the slot. His dreamskoot hummed into life. Snaffle slid into the saddle as quietly as he could. He pushed his thumb into the pad on his control panel.

Welcome, Snaffle, said the little screen. *Ready to go?*

Snaffle had never been so pleased to see those words. He gripped his handlebars and took a deep breath. "Power up! Lift off!" he ordered. He would have to rely on hover power for the first part of his escape. He dared not order "wings out" until he was clear of the baby owls. If they ripped through the delicate skin of the wings, he would be finished. Slowly, slowly, the dreamskoot began to rise out of the smelly nest.

The baby owls stopped fighting over the saddle cover and turned to look at him with their big eyes. They tilted their heads.

"Come on!" pleaded Snaffle as his dreamskoot slowly lifted into the air. "Hurry up!"

Poing!

One of the baby owls lunged forward and rapped its sharp beak against his helmet. Snaffle's head rang and he nearly fell off his dreamskoot.

Kerrang!

The second baby owl hit the engine casing and made a jagged scratch in the paintwork. The dreamskoot shuddered and lost height. Snaffle whimpered. Any minute now, one of the owls was going to pluck him from the saddle of his dreamskoot.

Kerrang! Poing! Kerrang! Poing! Kerrang!

Snaffle had had enough. He would have to risk it. "Wings out!" he yelled. As soon as the shimmering wings were fully unfolded, he opened the throttle. The dreamskoot shot away from the nest like a bullet. Snaffle headed for the round windows, leaving the baby owls squawking far below. He burst out into the night and took a big breath of fresh air. Now he had to get away before the mother owl came back.

Quickly, he turned on his D.R.E.A.M. and his map screen, his tracker and his dreamcom. The location of the gateway showed up on the map screen as a blue dot. Gratefully, Snaffle pointed his dreamskoot in the right direction and headed for home.

When he burst through the gateway a few minutes later, flanked by Cheroot and the Search and Rescue team in a V formation, the whole Dream Centre cheered. Cheroot gave him a salute and peeled off towards the Search and Rescue launch pads, followed by the rest of his team. Snaffle was left to land the dreamskoot on his own.

He groaned as he headed down to his own launch pad. There was a welcoming committee waiting for him. He could see Team Leader Flint standing with her hands behind her back. And there were

Midge, Vert and Harley, all waving madly. Snaffle scowled as he landed his dreamskoot. He knew they were only there to laugh at him. The filters had wiped him clean as he passed back through the gateway, so at least he was no longer covered in bits of owl poo and feathers, but he still smelt dreadful. His helmet was dented and his poor dreamskoot was scratched and battered.

Snaffle climbed from his saddle and his legs gave way beneath him. Team Leader Flint moved in like lightning and caught him before he hit the ground. Snaffle began to shake and his eyes filled up with tears. His humiliation was complete.

Midge, Vert and Harley hurried over. Snaffle waited for the jeering to start. But Midge gently eased off his helmet and smiled at him. Vert offered him a glass

of cool, fresh water. Harley looked at
him admiringly. "You beat an owl,
Snaffle! You must be some flyer!"

Snaffle looked up at Team Leader
Flint, waiting for the storm to start, but
she was looking at him proudly. "Well
done, Snaffle," she said. "Cool under
pressure. That's what I like to see in my
trainees." Her arm tightened around his
shoulders, holding him up.

Snaffle shook his head. "Why?" he said.

"Why what?" said Midge.

"Why are you all acting so pleased?"

"We're not acting!" said Midge. "We're really glad you made it."

Snaffle gave them a suspicious look.

"You are part of our dream team, Snaffle," said Vert.

"And that means you're family," said Harley, firmly. "That's what a dream team is. A family."

"You're not my family!" said Snaffle, but there was a lot less anger in his voice than usual.

"Whatever," grinned Harley.

"Right!" snapped Team Leader Flint. "Enough chat! We need to get this young man to the Infirmary!"

Team Leader Flint marched off. Snaffle followed, with Harley and Midge supporting him one on each side. Vert brought up the rear, carrying Snaffle's dented helmet as though it were a precious jewel.

A dream team was a family? What a stupid idea! Snaffle tried to sneer at the thought, but his lips refused to do what he wanted. They kept turning up at the corners instead. Snaffle smiled.